A MONSTER
IN THE MAILBOX

A MONSTER IN THE MAILBOX

BY SHEILA GORDON

ILLUSTRATED BY TONY DELUNA

E. P. DUTTON   NEW YORK

Text copyright © 1978 by Sheila Gordon
illustrations copyright © 1978 by Tony DeLuna

Library of Congress Cataloging in Publication Data

Gordon, Sheila.   A monster in the mailbox.

SUMMARY: The disappointment Julius experiences when
he buys a mail-order monster with his self-earned
money is not repeated when he buys a book of monster
fairy tales from a used-book store.
[1. Consumers—Fiction.   2. Reading—Fiction]
I. DeLuna, Tony.   II. Title.
PZ7.G65937Mo [Fic]   78-4600   ISBN: 0-525-35150-7

Published in the United States by E. P. Dutton, a Division
of Sequoia-Elsevier Publishing Company, Inc., New York
Published simultaneously in Canada by Clarke,
Irwin & Company Limited, Toronto and Vancouver

Editor: Ann Durell   Designer: Jennifer Dossin
Printed in the U.S.A.   First Edition
10 9 8 7 6 5 4 3 2 1

For David, Philippa, and Neil

CHAPTER 1

Once there was a boy called Julius. He had a brother, Buffington—called Buffy. And a sister, Elizabeth—called Lizzie.

But Julius was called Julius.

He was the youngest.

He had a dog called George, and a guppy called Lionel.

One day Julius' mother said, "Julius—your hair is getting to be too long in back. You'd better go to the barber."

"Not today," said Julius.

"*What's* happening today?" his mother asked.

"I have to go to the pet shop and see if I can find a new kind of food for my guppy."

"What's wrong with the old kind?"

"Well—I've been watching him swim around in

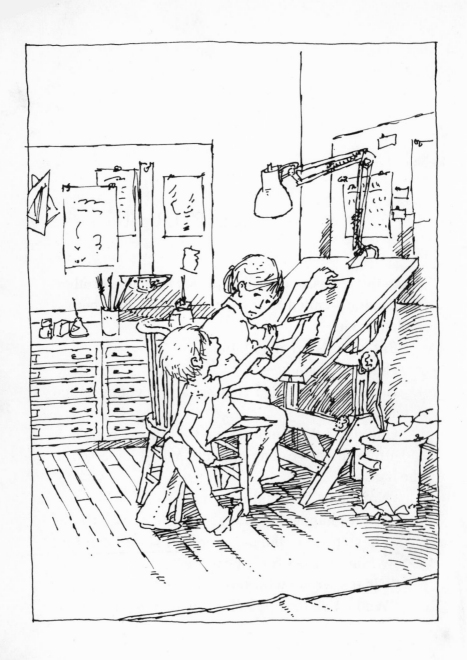

his tank for quite a while and it seems to me that he's losing weight. I think he must be tired of ants' eggs."

Julius came back from the pet shop very excited. He ran up the brownstone steps two at a time and slammed the front door shut and ran into the study where his mother was drawing a duckbill platypus. His mother was an illustrator for scientific journals; she had her drawing board set up in the study and did drawings of cells or snails, or whales or worms or ferns, or bones or stones, or mushrooms or minnows or whatever the scientists needed to illustrate what they wrote about; the duckbill platypus was for an article about Australia.

"MOM!"

"Oh Julius! Look what you made me do—you startled me and I jerked my arm and now my duckbill platypus looks like a duckbill shopping bag!"

"Mom!"

"*What* now, Julius?"

"Mom—could we get a boa constrictor for a pet?"

"A *What?*" said his mother, and she put down her pen and screwed the lid back on her bottle of black ink.

"A boa constrictor. There's a notice up in the window at the pet shop that someone is looking for a good home for a boa constrictor. *It's free!*"

His mother gave one more firm turn to the bottle lid and said, "No Julius. We definitely do not want to give a home to a boa constrictor. We do not want a boa constrictor for a pet. That's one thing I am very clear about in my mind."

"Why not?" Julius asked. "The man at the pet shop says they make very good pets."

Buffy came into the study just then. "What make very good pets?" he wanted to know.

"Boa constrictors," said Julius.

"Do they ever!" Buffy said. "My friend Benjamin has a pet boa constrictor. It lives in the bathtub, so everyone in the family has to take showers. *But*, their great-aunt from Sheboygan came to stay with them last week, and none of them remembered to warn her about it. So she walked into the bathroom, and when she saw that *huge* reptile curled up in the bathtub . . ."

"What happened?" Julius asked, his eyes round and wide open.

"She gave one really loud yell, and moved right out into a hotel, and she's refused to come anywhere near their place until they get rid of it. So Benjamin's mother told him he had to find another home for it. So . . . he's put up a notice in the pet shop about a free boa constrictor looking for a good home."

Lizzie walked into the study just then. "A free *what*?" she asked.

"A free boa constrictor," Buffy told her.

"There's this boa constrictor," their mother added, "that's looking for a good home. Julius feels we should offer ours."

"A *boa* constrictor!" Lizzie shuddered. "Do you know what boa constrictors *eat*?"

"What?" Julius asked.

"*Live mice*. You'd have to feed it *live mice*."

"Would you feed a teeny-weeny little mousie-wousie to a great big reptilian *beast*?" Buffy asked.

Everyone could see that Julius was starting to get mad.

"Don't be a tease, Buffy," their mother said.

But Julius looked very cross. "How about if a boa constrictor lives in the jungle and catches a mouse for food? There's nothing bad about that."

"That's different," Lizzie said, and did a few ballet turns around the room. "In the jungle all creatures have to fend for themselves. It's the law of the jungle. But it's inhuman"—she leaped across the rug and landed on one foot on the armchair with her arms held out like swan's wings—"to keep a boa constrictor living in a bathtub on a diet of live mice."

"A snake's not human," Julius shouted.

"But *you* are," Lizzie and Buffy said together. And as their mother could see that Julius was starting to get mad again, she asked them all what they thought of the duckbill platypus she was drawing, and they all admired it.

CHAPTER 2

A few days later, Buffy said he was going to the barber to get his hair cut, and he wondered if anyone whose hair was too long in back would like to come along with him.

"Not today," Julius said.

"*What's* happening today?"

"I've arranged to help Olly take his cat to the vet." Olly was Julius' best friend. His real name was Oliver.

"What's wrong with his cat?"

"It broke its jaw."

"Broke its jaw!" Buffy said. "How does a cat break its jaw?"

"Fell out of the window of their apartment. The vet said cats often break their jaws in summer—this

8

is the first case he's come across in winter. He put a little metal brace on its jaw. It's coming off today."

"That cat had better be extremely careful in the future," Buffy said.

"Why?"

"Because cats have nine lives, but now that one only has *eight* left."

So Julius and Olly put the cat in a cat box with a metal grid at one end for the cat to peer through and see where it was being taken, and caught the crosstown bus to the vet.

An old lady got on the bus and came and sat down beside them. The cat was sitting right up against the grid, looking very mad.

"What a dear little pussycat," she said.

Olly's cat hated riding on the bus, and she glared at the old lady out of great yellow eyes.

"Where are you taking your pussycat, boys?" the old lady asked.

"To the vet," they both said.

"Oh—poor little pussycat—is she feeling poorly —that's too bad. . . ." The old lady wiggled her finger in a friendly way in front of the grid. The cat let out an enormous yowl and settled down to making boiling noises, as if it was about to explode, and gave the

old lady such a turn that she moved away to another seat.

A young man in tall cowboy boots and a leather jacket and carrying a guitar came and sat down beside them. "Where you fellas takin' that cat?" he asked.

"To the vet."

"She ailin'?"

"Broke her jaw," Olly explained.

"No foolin'! How'd she manage that?"

"Fell out the window."

"How many floors?"

"Five."

"Whew!" The young man gave a low whistle. "Well—reckon she'd better take care now—only eight lives left. . . . Would you fellas be kind enough to inform me when we get to Atlantic Avenue? I'm a stranger in these here parts."

"This is Atlantic Avenue right now."

"Thank you, pardners." The young man got up and jumped off the bus just before the doors slid closed.

"Well now," said the vet after he removed the brace, "she'll be just fine. But she'll have to take it easy now—remember—she has only eight lives left."

That night Julius told his family if he had been that cat he would have bitten the very next person who said she only had eight lives left.

CHAPTER 3

The next evening, when Julius' father came home from work, he greeted his whole family and patted their dog, George, between the ears and said, "What's for dinner? I'm starving and it sure smells good in this kitchen." Then he said, "Julius—you look a fright."

"That's because he's so worried that his guppy is still losing weight," Buffy said.

Everyone could see that Julius was starting to get mad.

"Don't be a tease, Buffy," their father said. "Why you look a fright, Julius, is because you really do need to get your hair cut. You look shaggy. How can you see where you're going—it's so long in front."

"I guess I'll go and get it cut tomorrow. Oh—no —*not* tomorrow!"

"*What's* happening tomorrow?" his whole family asked.

"Olly's brother said if I came over to their place tomorrow, he'd let me try and play a tune on his French horn. He's already taught Olly the first three notes of 'Three Blind Mice.' "

"Planning to take up the French horn?" his mother asked as she tasted a sip of soup from a great steaming kettle.

"Mm-hmm . . ." Julius nodded, "I've been thinking about it—could I have a taste of that soup? Actually, what I really like most about the French horn is the way it curls around and around and it's made of such shiny brass and—"

"Do you know how hard it is to blow one, *single*, *solitary* sound out of a French horn?" Lizzie said.

"Be that as it may," their father said, "tomorrow you are *not* going to try your skill on any musical instrument whatever. Tomorrow—YOU ARE GOING TO THE BARBER."

"I guess I am," Julius said.

The next day, while Julius was waiting at the barbershop to get his hair cut, he looked at a few magazines and then at some comic books. When he came to the back cover of the last comic book in the pile, he saw an advertisement:

MONSTER! !

Send for our Monster now! !
Forty-eight inches tall
WALKING and TALKING MONSTER! !

Only $2.99.

Fill in name and address on coupon.
Satisfaction guaranteed or your money refunded.
SEND NOW for our
WALKING and TALKING MONSTER.

He read it twice through.

The cover had come loose, and while he was having his hair cut, Julius asked the barber, who was called Primo, if it would be all right for him to tear the coupon out.

"Sure—help yourself, kiddo," Primo said. "Take the whole cover if you like—feel free. . . ."

"Thank you, Primo," Julius said.

"You're very welcome, kiddo," Primo said. "Is that still too long in back?"

"It's just right," Julius said, still thinking about the monster.

When Julius got home he went straight to his room and opened his piggy bank. He counted up the dimes and nickels and cents that came rattling out. He found he had thirty-eight cents.

He went to look for his mother, who was in the

kitchen baking bread, and he asked her how he could earn some money, as he needed two dollars and ninety-nine cents very badly.

"What for?" his mother asked.

"I want to send away for a monster."

"Send away for a *what*?" his mother asked as she kneaded the dough.

"A monster," Julius said, and he showed her the advertisement on the comic-book cover.

His mother stopped kneading the dough, and read it, and then she said, "Well . . . honey . . . I doubt that it can be much of a monster for two dollars and ninety-nine cents. And your hair is still too long in back."

"How much *should* a really good monster cost?" Julius asked.

His mother cut up the dough into four pieces and told Julius that if he washed his hands he could put the loaves into the baking pans for her. So he washed his hands at the sink, and dried them, and while he was patting the dough into bread shapes, he asked his mother again, "How much *should* a really good monster cost?"

"Well . . ." his mother said, "I'm not actually too sure about that—but you're making that loaf too flat, Julius—do it gently—don't punch it—pat it."

18

After the loaves had risen in the pans and were baking in the oven and the whole house smelled of fresh bread—yeasty and warm and good—Julius was still wondering about the monster and how to earn some money so he could send away for it. He decided that he would have to find some jobs to do.

At dinner Julius said to his family, "I wish it would snow so I could go and clear some sidewalks and earn some money." But they were all watching his mother as she served rice pudding, which was their favorite dessert, and nobody paid him any attention.

"I need two dollars and ninety-nine cents very *badly*," he said, a little louder, "and I only have thirty-eight cents to my name."

"Pass me the nutmeg, Julius," Buffy asked, and he sprinkled nutmeg over his rice pudding.

"AREN'T THERE ANY JOBS I COULD DO AROUND THIS HOUSE TO EARN SOME MON-EY?" Julius asked in a very loud voice.

"You can stack the dishwasher," his father said, "but that's for love—not for money."

"You could walk George," Buffy said.

"But it's not my turn tonight."

"I know—it's mine—but I thought you wanted to earn some money. I will pay you a handsome sum."

"How much would I earn?"

"A dollar an hour—but it only takes five minutes to walk George."

Everyone could see that Julius was starting to get mad.

"Don't be a tease, Buffy," their father said.

While Julius stacked the dishwasher, he wondered how he would be able to earn enough money to send away for the monster.

Just then the phone rang. His mother answered and he heard her talking to Mrs. Kotzwinkle, their next-door neighbor. "I think Julius would be happy to do it," he heard his mother say, "he's in dire need of cash funds. I'll put him on. Julius," she called, "Mrs. Kotzwinkle wants to know if you'll be able to feed her cat this weekend—she's going to be out of town."

"Oh yes," Julius said. He went to the phone to talk to Mrs. Kotzwinkle.

"I'll drop the key in your mailbox before I go," she said, "and I'll leave cat food out on the kitchen counter. And will you give Sasha a bowl of canned food, a half bowl of dry food, and a bowl of water? No milk."

"Why not?" Julius asked. "I thought cats love milk."

"They do," said Mrs. Kotzwinkle, "but it's bad for them—no milk—right?"

"Right."

"Many of the things we love are bad for us," Mrs. Kotzwinkle said.

"But a whole lot of them are good for us too," Julius remarked.

"Like what, for instance?" she asked.

"Like rice pudding. Right?"

"Right," said Mrs. Kotzwinkle.

Julius went back to stacking the dishwasher. He hoped he would earn enough from the Kotzwinkles to send away for the monster.

Just then Lizzie came into the kitchen to get a glass of milk. She was in the middle of her French homework and she said that French always made her very thirsty.

"Did you know that milk is bad for cats?" Julius asked her.

"That's news to me," she answered.

"Mrs. Kotzwinkle says it's very bad for them."

"Well it's good for me," Lizzie said. She wiped away a milk moustache with the back of her hand. "Cats don't have problems like French homework...."

On Saturday evening Julius let himself into the Kotzwinkles' house with the key they had dropped off. There were no lights on, and the place felt empty and strange. It was very quiet. Julius thought it was a bit scary. He couldn't see the cat anywhere.

He called, "Sasha . . . Sasha . . ." but she didn't appear. He found the light switch in the hall and turned on a few lights. On the kitchen counter there were some cans of cat food and a box of dry food and three small bowls.

He filled up the bowls with the right amount of food and water, then went and stood in the kitchen doorway calling, "Sasha . . . Sasha . . . kitty-kitty-kitty . . . puss-puss-puss . . ." the way Mr. Kotzwinkle always called in the garden at night when he wanted Sasha to come indoors.

But all remained silent.

He called, "Sasha—come and get your dinner . . . dinnertime Sasha. . . ."

Suddenly something dropped through the air in an arc past his shoulder and thudded onto the kitchen table.

"HELP!" shouted Julius.

He turned his head very slowly, very scared, to see what it was.

It was Sasha, sitting on the kitchen table, neatly washing her face; she had been watching him from the top of the cabinet and had leaped down onto the table.

"Sasha! You really had me scared for a moment!"

She jumped to the floor and wound herself around and about Julius' ankles, purring loudly.

"You are a *bad* cat," Julius said, "hiding away like that and almost frightening me out of my wits."

He stroked her white shirtfront, and she purred as if a small motor were turned on somewhere inside her. Her paws were all white; except for her shirtfront and socks, she was pure black.

"Yes, Sasha . . . almost out of my wits," he said, rubbing her silky black ears. "Now come and eat."

She ate most of the canned food, crunched a few bits of the dried food, and drank a lot of the water, lapping delicately with her neat pink tongue.

"You know what's good for you—don't you, Sasha?" Julius said.

He lay down on the floor beside the cat and tried to examine exactly how her tongue managed to throw the water to the back of her throat, as he thought it must be quite difficult to drink without lips. But Sasha stopped lapping and licked his chin instead, and he was surprised at how raspy her tongue felt, as if it were made of fine sandpaper.

Then she lost interest in him and began to wash her face. She licked her paw and wiped one cheek, licked it again and wiped the other, and then got to work on the spot between her ears. Julius liked the

25

way cats were so neat and liked to be clean even though they never got to see what they looked like.

He wondered what cats thought about—a lot of the time he knew exactly what his dog George thought about—but cats kept their thoughts to themselves. When George pulled his leash down from the hook where it hung, it meant he was thinking about going for a walk; when he put his head on your lap, it meant he was thinking about how he liked you. Dogs were much easier to figure out than cats.

Sasha came to the front door with Julius when it was time for him to go, and he felt sorry to leave her all alone in the empty house. "I'll see you first thing in the morning, Sasha, okay?" he told her, and he carefully checked that the door was securely locked. As he went down the steps, he saw Sasha sitting in the window, very still, like a statue of an Egyptian cat he had seen in the Metropolitan Museum.

On Sunday morning, when Julius went to feed Sasha, she was waiting for him just inside the front door and seemed quite pleased to see him. He stayed to play with her awhile after she had eaten. He made her a toy by crumpling a piece of aluminum foil into a ball, and she chased it all around the kitchen and into the living room. Suddenly she discovered her

26

own tail and tried to chase that. Noticing that wherever she went it followed her, she became so scared that she dashed across the living room and disappeared up the fireplace chimney.

"Sasha!" Julius yelled up the chimney, "come right down you crazy little cat." He felt quite worried—what would he say to the Kotzwinkles if Sasha was stuck up the chimney? He wondered if he would have to call the fire department to get her down. "Sasha! Come right down, will you!"

After a while, the tip of her tail appeared, and then the rest of her, coming down backwards. She sat down on the hearth and calmly started to wash her face.

"Whew!" Julius ran the back of his hand over his forehead. "What a relief! Sasha—you had me worried for a while."

On Sunday evening Mrs. Kotzwinkle popped round to collect her key and pay Julius.

"Sasha looks very content," she said. "I hope she didn't give you any trouble."

"Apart from scaring me out of my wits twice," he said, "she was no trouble at all."

He told Mrs. Kotzwinkle what Sasha had done, and she boomed with laughter. Her dangling earrings and all her bracelets shook and tinkled, and all

27

her rings flashed and twinkled. Julius laughed too. He really liked Mrs. Kotzwinkle.

She dabbed her eyes with a small purple handkerchief. "Well—" she said, "that's the feline species for you! An endless source of fascination—right Julius?"

"Right," Julius said.

She paid him three dollars and left.

CHAPTER 4

Now Julius had enough money to send away for a monster.

On Monday, as soon as he got in from school, he asked his mother if it was all right just to put the money in an envelope with the coupon and send them off.

His mother said she didn't think that a mail-order monster was such a great idea, but it was his money. If that was what he wanted to do with it, she guessed the best way would be for him to give her the money and she would write out a check for him to mail. That would be a whole lot easier than trying to stuff dollar bills and nickels and pennies and dimes into an envelope.

Julius brought Mrs. Kotzwinkle's three dollars to

his mother, and she wrote out a check for two dollars and ninety-nine cents.

"Now I owe you one penny," she said.

"Oh—keep the change," Julius said.

He filled out his name and address on the coupon. He addressed the envelope very neatly and carefully, his tongue following the movements of his fingers as they wrote. Then he put the coupon and check in the envelope, sealed it, and stuck on a stamp. He whistled for George, clipped on his leash, and they went out to the mailbox to mail the letter.

"How long do you think it will take for a monster to get here?" he asked Lizzie.

But Lizzie was practicing a waltz at the piano and not really listening to him, and she just answered, "ONE—two—three—ONE—two—three—oh—years and years I guess—ONE—two—three, TRA—la—la . . ."

"How long do you think it will take for a monster to get here?" he asked Buffy.

But Buffy, who was standing on the desk fitting a new bulb into the light, put a monster expression on his face. He growled and made his hands into claws. He jumped up and down on the desk, grunting

in a deep, monsterish voice, "The monster is here already—watch out for the MONSTER!"

Then he jumped down off the desk and chased Julius all around the house, growling and roaring. Julius shouted, "Help! Help!"

Their mother told them that the cake she had just put in the oven would sink as flat as a pancake if they went on creating such a racket.

In the evening, after dinner, when Julius had done his homework and taken a bath and brushed his teeth, he went into the study to say good night to his father.

His father was writing at the desk. He was a professor of archeology and was preparing a lecture for his students about the Pueblo cliff dwellings of Arizona.

"Dad—how long do you think it would take a monster to get here?" he asked.

"Depends on where it's coming from," his father said.

Julius remembered the address he had written on the envelope. "From Fresno, California."

"Oh—that would take quite a while, son, quite a while. . . ." his father told him.

CHAPTER 5

Every afternoon, when Julius was walking home from school, he wondered if his monster had arrived yet.

How would it come?

Would it be unloaded, in a cage, from the back of an enormous truck? Would it be rattling the bars and growling, with old Mrs. Robinson across the street peeking worriedly through the curtains?

Would it come in a huge crate, with its eye peering out through an air hole?

Would it be tied up in a sack?

Would the mailman be carrying it?

How would it fit into the mailbox?

WOULD THE MONSTER BE CARRYING THE MAILMAN?

He would run up the front steps of his house and

open the front door and yell, "Hi Mom—has my monster come?"

But every day his mother would answer, "No, Julius—it's not here yet."

"Julius," Olly asked him one day after school, "what's the big rush to get home so fast every day?"

"I have to check the mail—I'm expecting an important delivery."

"What is it?" Olly wanted to know.

But Julius just looked mysterious. "You'll find out in good time" was all he would tell Olly.

On Saturdays, when there was no school, Julius, with George beside him, would watch out the window for the mailman or a delivery truck.

Whenever a truck pulled up outside his house, he was quite sure it must be to deliver the monster. But it never was. It might be a delivery of clay for Mrs. Kotzwinkle, who was a potter and had a potter's wheel and kiln in the basement of her house. Or it was a new washing machine for Mrs. O'Halloran, who had five children and whose washing machine was always breaking down even though Mr. O'Halloran was a plumber. Or it was a few cases of wine for Osgood Austin Auchincloss, the famous poet who lived across the street—though Lizzie said no one *she* knew had ever heard of him, so how famous could he be? Or it might be a few bags of topsoil for old Mr. Popolizio, in the house at the corner, to put in his backyard vegetable garden where he grew prize tomatoes and giant squash. He used to work at the docks unloading crates from ships until he hurt his back when something fell on him from a crane. His wife said she was going to write a recipe book called *Seventeen Hundred Different Ways To Cook Tomatoes and Squash.*

But whatever it was—it never was the monster.

After a while, Julius got tired of expecting the monster.

It was getting to be spring, and the gray ice, packed in frozen mounds all along the sidewalks, was turning soft and spongy. Puddles formed that reflected the sky.

Lizzie called them all to the window to see the two blue jays that came every spring to their garden. The whole family watched the blue flash of their wings as they swooped about the garden and settled on the bare trees.

"I wonder why such pretty birds have such grating, screeching voices," Lizzie said.

"That's the way it goes, I guess," their father said.

Julius wondered what that meant: That's the way

it goes. That's the way *what* goes? he puzzled. And whatever *it* is, which way does it go?

Soon the weather was so fine that everyone was impatient to be outdoors. Every day after school, Julius and Olly would go and play Frisbee in the park. Julius would dash into the house, drop his book bag on the floor of his room, grab a glass of milk and a peanut-butter-and-bean-sprouts-and-cheddar-cheese-and-tuna-salad-and-tomato-on-rye sandwich —or whatever other four or five fillings he found in the refrigerator that could be fitted between two slices of rye bread without dislocating his jaw. He would yell to his mother that he was going to play in the park, and pick up his Frisbee, and run off to meet Olly.

He didn't think too much about the monster anymore, and only sometimes remembered to ask his mother if there was any mail for him. On days when he was tired or cranky or had too much homework or had had an argument with Olly or thought his teacher had been mean, he would go straight to the study where his mother worked at her drawing board, dump his book bag on the rug, and say in a cross voice, "I guess there was nothing for me in the mail today...."

CHAPTER 6

One day Julius came home from school and ran into his bedroom to get his Frisbee. There, lying in the middle of his bed, was a small, square package.

He picked it up and saw his name and address on the label.

It came from the Acme Novelty Company in Fresno, California.

It was wrapped in brown paper stuck down with gummed tape, and tied up with string.

He held it in the palm of his hand.

It did not feel very heavy. . . .

In fact—it felt rather light.

He took it to show his mother, who was busy working on a drawing of the webbed toes of the Javanese flying frog.

"What's this?" he asked her. "It was on my bed."

"Well . . . it came for you in the mail this morning. . . ." She stopped drawing, and they both looked at the rather small, square package.

"Hmm—I wonder what it could be," Julius said. "I *was* expecting a monster, but this couldn't be it— a monster couldn't fit into a box as small as this . . . could it?" he asked his mother.

"I'm not sure, really, honey . . . um . . . why not open it and see what it is," his mother said.

So Julius took his mother's scissors and cut the string.

Then he pulled off the gummed tape.

Then he unwrapped the brown wrapping paper.

Then he opened up the stiff cardboard box.

Then he took out of the box a flippy-flappy, rolled up, rubbery, flubbery, red thing, and unrolled it, and spread it out on the floor.

He and his mother both looked at it.

It was nearly as long as Julius.

It was nearly as wide as Julius.

It was made of thick red rubber.

It was shaped like an enormous peanut or a small snowman.

It had a face painted on the small round end.

It had a tie and six buttons painted on the large round end.

It had two shoes painted at the bottom.

It had a tube, like a bicycle tire has, stuck in at the side.

It lay flat and red and rubbery on the floor, looking up at Julius and his mother.

Julius and his mother looked down at it. Then they looked at each other.

Then Julius' chin began to wobble. And his lips began to tremble. And his eyes began to fill with tears. And Julius burst out crying.

"It's my *monster*," he cried.

His mother took him onto her lap and held him while he cried. She also looked rather sad about the monster.

After Julius had cried for a while, she gave him her handkerchief, and he wiped his eyes and blew his nose.

"Well, now . . ." his mother said. "Let's take a look at it, anyway. I think it's supposed to be blown up."

So they went to look for Buffy to ask him to pump it up with his bicycle pump.

"What *is* it?" Buffy wanted to know.

42

"It's my monster," Julius said, and a few more tears rolled down his cheeks.

"Well—" Buffy said, "let's pump it up and see what's supposed to happen, anyway."

So they put the pump into the small tube in the monster's side. They took turns at pumping and pumping. Lizzie came along to see what it was all about, and so did George, their dog.

It puffed up and swelled out and grew bigger and bigger until it was like a small, roly-poly, jolly clown. When it was all filled up with air, they stopped pumping and closed the valve.

Then Julius stood it up and said to everyone, "Ssh—ssh—wait."

When George came sniffing around the monster's feet to check if it was a friend or an enemy, Julius said, "*Stop* that, George! Ssh everyone . . . wait . . . *quiet*. . . ."

"What are we waiting *for*?" Lizzie asked.

"Ssh . . . it's supposed to walk and talk," Julius told her. "It's a walking and talking monster."

Julius' mother and Lizzie and Buffy all looked at each other, but they didn't say anything.

They all waited.

George sat down and waited too, very curious, with his left ear cocked up.

But the monster didn't talk.

Not one sound.

And it didn't walk.

Not one step.

It just slowly toppled over, and lay on its side on the kitchen floor.

Julius looked as if he was starting to cry again. So Buffy picked up the monster and punched it down and said, "Rotten old monster—why won't you walk or talk—a fine walking and talking monster *you've* turned out to be!" The monster bounced about and fell over and bounced up again.

Lizzie caught it and said, "Oh monster—may I have the next dance?" and waltzed about the place with the monster. "ONE, two, three; ONE, two, three."

George began to chase the monster and yap excitedly and snap at its feet, and Julius began to laugh. They all romped about, wrestling with the monster and shouting and bouncing it around the room— when suddenly—there was a very loud BANG!!!

George ran away and hid behind the sofa.

And there on the floor lay a large flat piece of torn red rubber.

And no more monster.

Julius cried.

George came out from behind the sofa and whined.

Buffy said, "What a rotten old monster *that* turned out to be."

Lizzie said, "Oh well . . ." And they all stood about looking at the exploded monster, and George went and sniffed suspiciously at it.

And Julius cried.

After a while Lizzie said, "Julius . . . would you like to have a go at my new mosaic tile set?" which was very kind of her as she had just got it for her birthday and hadn't used it herself yet.

But Julius was very mad now, and he yelled.

"It didn't even WALK. And it didn't TALK. And it wasn't FORTY-EIGHT INCHES TALL EITHER!"

His mother said, "I'm sorry, darling—it's a big disappointment, I know. . . ."

Lizzie said, "Are you coming or aren't you, Julius? You can tile a candy dish if you like."

So Julius went to Lizzie's room and she showed him how to fit all the little colored tiles with cement and grout to make a candy dish.

Their mother said to Buffy, "Better put this poor

old monster outside in the garbage, Buff—he'll get upset all over again if he sees it lying around."

So that was the end of the monster.

Julius was very quiet for the rest of the afternoon and the evening. Olly called, and Julius told his mother to tell him that he didn't feel like coming out to play.

He made a nice red and blue and yellow candy dish with Lizzie's mosaic tile set. But he was very quiet.

His father came home and they had dinner. After dinner they all ate some candy that their mother served in the candy dish. But Julius was very quiet.

Then he did his homework. He took a bath and brushed his teeth. He said good night to his family and went to bed.

In the middle of the night, Julius' mother woke up. She lay awake in the dark wondering what had woken her.

Then she heard a strange sound.

Tik tik tiktiktik tik.

She woke Julius' father. "Can you hear a strange sound?" she asked him.

He sat up in bed and listened.

Tiktik tik tik tiktiktiktiktik.

48

"I wonder what it is," he said.

So they both got out of bed and followed the strange sound until they came to the study.

The light was on in the study.

Tik tik tiktiktik tik.

Julius was sitting at the desk in the study, in his pajamas, typing.

"Julius!" his mother said. "What on earth are you doing?"

"Julius!" his father said. "It's way past midnight!"

Julius looked up at them and went right on with his typing.

Tik tik tik tik tik tiktik.

"I'm writing a letter," Julius said.

"Who to?" his mother and father asked together.

"To the monster people," Julius said.

"Can't it wait till morning?" his mother asked.

"NO!" Julius said.

By then Buffy and Lizzie had also woken, and so had George, and they all came to the study to see what the fuss was about.

"He's writing a letter to the monster people," their father told them.

Tiktik tik tiktiktiktiktik. Julius typed away, taking no notice at all of his family.

"Well . . ." his mother said, "we're all going back to bed. . . . Make sure and turn off the lights when you're through writing that letter, Julius."

But Julius just typed away.

Tik tik tiktiktik.

The next day was Saturday, and at breakfast Julius showed them all his monster letter.

It went like this:

> Dear Sir,
> Yester   day I receeved a monster.
> There were a few things wrong with it:
> Its ~~neck~~ head did not touch its body.
> It was not 48 inches tall.
> It did not talk. Or walk.
> And it ~~pooped~~ poped   a few minutes after
> I got it.
> I would like my money back.
> From,
Julius

His mother and father looked at each other across the breakfast table, and they both said they thought it was a good letter.

"Quite right," Lizzie said, "that'll teach them. . . ."

And after breakfast Buffy helped Julius address the envelope and stick on a stamp, and they put George on the leash and went off to mail the letter.

CHAPTER 7

In a dusty little office in a warehouse in Fresno, California, a secretary called Iris was sitting at her desk. All around her, from the floor to the ceiling, were shelves filled with cardboard cartons. The cartons were all labeled. There were labels like:

Vampire Blood   (fake blood; real-looking, scary, 79¢)

Rubber Masks   (with hair—Savage Monster, Fierce Gorilla, Horrible Frankenstein, $1.99)

Joke Bubble Gum   (Hot pepper; Scorching; Garlic flavor; Vile, 25¢)

Monster Record   (eerie; supernatural; howling banshees; groans; terrifying thunderstorms; maniacal screams; hideous laughter; many more, 89¢)

Lifelike Mouse   (crawls, creeps up sleeve; scare your friends, 39¢)

555 Insults   (put-downs for all occasions, 59¢)

There was a knock at the door, and the mailman came in with a bundle of letters.

Iris opened the letters, put them in a wire basket, and took them to another office.

"Mail's come, Fred," she said, and put the letters down on the desk.

Fred looked through the pile of mail. Then he said, "Kid here wants his money back. Send him the regular reply."

A few days later, Julius received a letter from the Acme Novelty Company, Fresno, California.

It said:

Dear Sir/Madam,

As you are not satisfied with the goods you received, you may order anything else from our catalogue to the value of $5.00.

Catalogue enclosed.

Yours truly,
Acme Novelty Company

Julius showed the letter and catalogue to Buffy and Lizzie.

"Wow—five dollars . . ." Buffy said.

"Let's see what else you could get," Lizzie said. "How about a full-length sixteen-inch ventriloquist's

dummy with controls to operate mouth and move head?''

"Or how about," Buffy suggested, "some vampire blood and a magnet that lifts fifty pounds of solid steel?''

"Or a bargain bag of popular tricks, and a thousand tiny magnets?''

"Or a flesh-eating plant—bites finger, eats flies and meat, snaps shut on anything: finger, pencil, bugs?''

"Or five hundred and fifty-five insults—put-downs for all occasions?''

"Or a pocket spy telescope?''

Buffy and Lizzie were reading from the catalogue with such interest that neither of them noticed that Julius was getting madder, and madder, and madder. Suddenly he opened his mouth and yelled, "I DON'T WANT ANYTHING FROM THEIR ROTTEN OLD CATALOGUE! NOTHING! I ONLY WANT MY MONEY BACK! They said in the advertisement, 'Satisfaction guaranteed or your money refunded,' and I'M NOT SATISFIED ONE BIT WITH THEIR ROTTEN OLD MONSTER!''

"So write and tell them," Lizzie said.

She gave him back the catalogue and he dropped it in the wastepaper basket and sat down at the typewriter.

Tik tiktiktik tik tiktiktiktiktik.

> Dear Sir,
> I am not satisfied with that monster.
> I don't want anything else.
> I would like my money back.
>
> > From,
> > Julius

Buffy told him how to spell *satisfied*.

Back in the dusty office in Fresno, California, Iris opened the letter from Julius and took it in to Fred.

"Kid just wants his money back, Fred," she told him.

Fred put out his hand for the letter, read it, and shrugged his shoulders.

"So send it to him," he said.

CHAPTER 8

So Julius received a check for two dollars and ninety-nine cents.

He showed it to George, who sniffed curiously at it and then tried to chew it.

He showed it to his guppy Lionel, but Lionel was diving about the aquarium picking up bits of his new fish food, and looked to Julius as if he were concentrating on putting on a little weight.

He showed it to Buffy.

He showed it to Lizzie.

He showed it to his mother, and she changed it into three single dollar bills for him. "Keep the change," she said.

And then Julius and Buffy and Lizzie and George all went off to the shops.

"Where are you four going?" their mother called out the window.

"We're going with Julius to spend his monster money—we're going to try the bookstore first," Lizzie answered, as Buffy and Julius tried to pull George away from a large English sheepdog who was his enemy.

George waited outside the bookstore for them, with his leash tied around a fire hydrant. Every time anyone came out the door his tail began to wag and he looked to see if it was his family.

They were such a long time that he got tired of standing and he lay down on the sidewalk beside the hydrant, with his head resting on his paws and his eyes never moving from the doorway of the store.

The reason that they were such a while was that it was their favorite store. An old sign above the window was painted with faded letters that said:

BOOKS
BOUGHT AND SOLD
USED—SECONDHAND
RARE—ANTIQUARIAN—OUT OF PRINT
BOOK FIND SERVICE

The store was filled with old and used and secondhand books which crowded the shelves and

stood piled on tables and overflowed from boxes onto the floor. There was a smell of books and dust and old yellowing papers. Some of the books were so old that the pages crumbled and flaked when they were turned over. The old bookseller didn't mind how long they spent browsing through piles and shelves and boxes and cartons filled with old books, just so long as they put them back in the right place after they had looked at them.

"Put them back just where you took'them from," he would say in a growly voice as soon as they walked in.

He had white hair and thick eyeglasses and he liked anyone who liked books—so long as they put them back in the right place.

"Can you tell me—" he would ask them, "if it's any *easier*—if it's any *less* trouble—to put a book back in the *wrong* place? Of course it isn't—yet that's what the majority of the public does nevertheless...."

His wife was a small lady whose job was putting the books back in the right place. All day she tidied books away.

Once Julius heard her sigh a very big sigh for such a small person. He'd said, "I guess it must be pretty hard to try and keep so many hundreds and hundreds of books tidy."

She'd smiled at him and said, "You're not kidding, sweetheart—it's one of those jobs that just goes on forever . . . but at least they're books. Now if they were cans of soup, or boxes of shoes, or bottles of pills—then I'd really have something to complain about."

Julius and Buffy and Lizzie sat down on some old wooden crates. They picked up books to look through from stacks piled all around them, without having to move from where they sat. It was nice and warm and musty and dusty sitting on a crate and leafing through old books.

"If I were you, I'd get this book," Buffy said. "It's all about how there's another ice age due in ten thousand years."

"How many years?" Julius asked.

"Ten thousand."

"Ten *thousand!* Whew! You had me worried for a moment," Julius said.

The old bookseller came by, balancing a pile of books that reached up as high as his forehead. "Having a good time, kids?" his voice came out from behind the books.

"Yes," they all said.

"Put them all back just where you took them from," he said, and disappeared behind some bookshelves.

"Maybe I should get this," Julius said.

He showed them a limp yellow book called *How to Play the French Horn in Ten Easy Lessons.* Buffy and Lizzie just looked at him as if to say "What next?" So he put it back just where he had taken it from.

"You should get this book about wolves," Lizzie said. "It looks really good. It says here that wolves aren't fierce animals at all—they're actually very kind and don't attack human beings as is commonly believed."

"You should get this book about life on other planets," Buffy said. "It says here that if there is life on other planets, they will have to get in touch with us first."

"Why?" Lizzie and Julius asked.

"Because they will have to be technologically more advanced than we are. It says here that we're not advanced enough to make contact with them first."

Julius wondered who *they* were.

"Here's a book called *How to Take Care of Your Guppy*," Julius said. "I wonder if it says what to do if your guppy's losing weight."

But his brother and sister gave him their "What next?" look and didn't answer.

"You should get this," Lizzie said. She held out an old blue leather book with gold lettering, called *Oliver Twist* by Charles Dickens. Then she put it back and said, "Oh—I guess maybe not—it really made me cry a lot when I read it. You can read it when you're older."

"You should get this book about insects," Buffy said. "The pictures are really neat. Look—there are potter wasps that make little clay bottles to lay their eggs in—we'll have to tell Mrs. Kotzwinkle about that. . . ."

"I'd get this if it was *my* money," Lizzie said. She showed them a book of Victorian dollhouses, furnished with little carpets and cushions and curtains and small iron stoves with tiny pots and pans on them. Dolls were sitting on miniature armchairs or playing the piano or putting babies to sleep in small cradles.

Julius said, "I'm having a hard time making up my mind. . . ."

"Take your time, sweetheart," the bookseller's wife said. "We stay open till seven tonight."

At last they chose a book. Outside, George was getting to be quite impatient, as if he thought they'd forgotten him and gone home without him. He was pulling at his leash and complaining in short woof-ish barks.

Julius went over to the counter carrying under his arm a big old book with a red leather cover and gold lettering. It was called *The Monster Book of Fairy Tales*. The pages were of heavy paper, and each story had a brightly colored picture page. There were pictures of castles and witches and dragons and giants and forests with trees shaped like monsters, and even the clouds in the skies were strange and eerie shapes.

They all agreed that it was the book to buy, but they thought it would cost much more than Julius had.

"How much is this book of fairy tales?" Julius asked the old bookseller.

"This is quite a valuable old book," he said, looking through it.

Julius felt quite worried, as he very much wanted to have it.

The old man stared at him through the thick lenses of his glasses.

"Is it more than three dollars?" Julius asked.

"You have three dollars to spend on a book?" the old man asked.

Julius nodded his head.

"Well—by a strange coincidence, this book costs exactly three dollars—including tax."

"Whew!" Julius said. "You had me quite worried for a moment."

"Would you like it wrapped?" the old man asked.

"No thank you," Julius said.

"A true reader," the old man told them. "In my more than forty years' experience as a rare and secondhand book dealer, I have found that the true reader never wants the book he has bought to be packaged. He wants to hold it in his hand, to feel its weight and the texture of its cover in his palm. He wants to carry it straight home and start reading it. Right?"

They all felt pleased that they were true readers, as they never wanted him to wrap the books they bought from him. "Right," they said.

George was very happy to see them, and he stood up and wagged his tail. When they unleashed him from the fire hydrant, he put his front paws on them and licked their hands and faces, and they all went home.

Julius went straight to his room and lay down on his stomach on the bed and opened his book of fairy tales.

And the first story he read was about two children who were lost in a dark forest and were found by an ugly old witch in a black dress and pointed hat, who wouldn't let them go. It was really scary until at last they managed to push the wicked witch into the oven and find their way back home with their pockets filled with the witch's pearls and precious stones.

Then he read another story about a lovely young girl called Beauty, who was forced to live in a castle with a frightful beast. She became so fond of the hairy, ugly creature that, in the end, because of her kindness to him, there was a blaze of light and fireworks crackled and rockets exploded and fireflies danced in the air, and the beast turned into a prince and married Beauty.

And then Lizzie popped her head around the door and said, "Julius—dinner's nearly ready."

"Coming..." Julius answered, but he turned over the page and kept reading until Buffy came into the room and said, "How's that book?"

Julius said, "It's great—look at this picture...."

They both looked at a picture of an ugly black wolf with red eyes and long fanged teeth, all dressed up in a nightgown and cap, springing out of bed towards a frightened-looking little girl.

"Scary—isn't it?" Julius said.

"Mm-hmm—" Buffy agreed. "But you must come and eat now."

"I'll be right there," Julius said, without even looking up from the book. And he read until his father came into the room and said, "Julius! Dinner is on the table and here you are still lying on your bed and you haven't even washed your hands yet."

"Sorry Dad—I'll be right there. But just take a look at this book I bought with the monster money."

His father sat down on the bed beside him. Julius showed him the pictures of glass mountains and golden roads and a boy no bigger than your thumb, who saves his whole family from a wicked ogre.

They were both looking at a picture of a dwarf who could change straw into gold when the door opened and Julius' mother walked in. "What's going on here?" she asked. "Dinner's getting cold."

"Sorry—" his father said. "It's this book that Julius bought with his monster money—have you seen it?"

"I'll look at it *after* dinner," his mother said. "I've spent all afternoon drawing cross-section diagrams of the way beavers build dams, with hundreds and hundreds of small twigs and branches. Also I had to draw a lot of sand particles and blades of grass. So right now, the only thing that really interests me is a plate of steaming lamb stew."

69

"We'll be right there," his father said. "Julius,
go and wash your hands."

At last they all sat down to dinner.

"Julius—don't gobble your food like that," his
father said.

"What's the rush?" his mother asked.

"Well—I want to get back to my book. There's
this story I want to read about a dragon all covered
with shiny green scales and when he breathes,"
Julius said, "when he breathes—streams of fire and
smoke come pouring out of his nostrils and his eyes
blaze and whole forests and villages burn down. . . ."

"Sounds better than a red rubber old imitation
mail-order monster that pops after you've had it
about five minutes," Buffy said.

"Oh," Julius said, and he started to eat his
rutabaga more slowly, "it is—much better!"

SHEILA GORDON grew up in Johannesburg, South Africa, and now lives in Brooklyn, New York. Remembering a disappointment her younger son experienced when he was eight, she was prompted to write *A Monster in the Mailbox*. "With high expectations, he ordered a 'real, live' monster advertised by a mail-order house. He was bitterly disappointed by what he received. It was his first encounter with the 'real' world, in contrast to the world of the possibilities of the imagination."

TONY DELUNA is a native New Yorker who has long been intrigued by children's books and comic strips. His personal collection at one time included over 500 rare children's books and 2500 comic books! For many years he was the art director of the juvenile books division of a publishing house. Recently he supervised the production of *American Comic Strips* (Hyperion Press), a series dealing with comic strips of the early 1900s. The father of three, Tony DeLuna has illustrated several books for children.